**"Why, those are 'other way-around' pills!"
Albert, Miss Know It All's brother, said.**

One glance had been enough for Albert to tell. "I hope nobody's been fooling with them," he added soberly.

The girls all began to shake their heads.

"I know *now* what they are," Miss Know It All said to Albert, "but I just found out a moment ago. Mr. Not So Much ate one, and he's—well—" Her voice drifted off.

Albert looked very interested. "He's gone the other-way-around?"

"I'm afraid so," Miss Know It All answered.

"Oh, my, my, my." Miss Lavender felt faint. She sat down in a heap on the sofa.

Miss Plum quieted the little girls, who were beginning to whisper among themselves. "Let me understand this," she said. "Mr. Not So Much has eaten one of these pills and—"

"Only part of one," Miss Lavender murmured faintly.

"Yes, that's right, only part of one," Miss Plum agreed. "He threw what was left of the pill into the fire, and the fire went out."

"Naturally," said Albert with an elegant and handsome shrug. "Even fires can go the other-way-around."

Miss Know It All Returns

by Carol Beach York

Illustrated by Victoria de Larrea

A BANTAM SKYLARK BOOK®
TORONTO · NEW YORK · LONDON · SYDNEY · AUCKLAND

For Mother,
my most faithful reader

RL 5, 008–012

MISS KNOW IT ALL RETURNS
*A Bantam Book / published by arrangement with
the Author*
Bantam Skylark edition / September 1985

ISBN 0-553-15351-X

Published simultaneously in the United States and Canada

PRINTED IN THE UNITED STATES OF AMERICA

CW   0 9 8 7 6 5 4 3 2

Contents

1

Miss Know It All Returns

Miss Know It All returned to Butterfield Square on a spring day. She had first arrived at Number 18—*The Good Day Orphanage for Girls*—on a spring day. And it was on a spring day that she came again.

A year had gone by, yet everything looked just the same as she stepped along the sidewalk and turned in at the gate of Number 18. The Square looked just the same. And all the old brick houses with their neat lawns and black iron fences were just the same.

Miss Know It All herself was just the same. Her hat was clamped on securely, and her black patent-leather pocketbook was as shiny as new shoes.

It was Saturday afternoon. The twenty-eight girls of The Good Day were playing here and there about the yard and in the house—and a great cry went up when they saw that their dear, dear friend Miss Know It All had returned.

Kate saw her first, and fell out of a tree in surprise.

Phoebe saw her next, and her bubble of gum—one of the biggest she had ever blown—broke and stuck all over her mouth and chin.

Tatty saw her, and tried to pull up her stockings and brush back her hair as she ran to welcome her.

Elsie May saw her, and her eyes flew wide open. She forgot to be dignified, and she ran as fast as the smaller girls.

Mary saw her and Elizabeth saw her and Jane saw her!

Little Ann came running with jam on her face and a dandelion in her hair.

By the time Miss Know It All was halfway up the front walk, she was surrounded by girls clamoring around her, until the whole procession looked like a jumping, bumping cluster coming toward the front door.

Miss Lavender and Miss Plum, the two ladies in charge of The Good Day, were in the parlor. They were roused by all the commotion outside and went to the window.

"Why, it's Miss Know It All!" Miss Plum announced to Miss Lavender.

"My, my, my," Miss Lavender exclaimed. She peered out over the gold rims of her spectacles as Miss Know It All came

up the walk amid the throng of little girls.

Miss Plum, quick and efficient, was already on her way to the front door to greet the visitor. Miss Lavender patted her fluffy white curls, perked up the ruffle on her collar, and scurried after Miss Plum on her plump little legs.

Miss Plum was tall and thin, with legs much longer and faster than Miss Lavender's, and she was already far ahead.

Even Cook had stuck her head out of the kitchen to see what all the noise was about.

When Miss Know It All had first come to Butterfield Square, she had introduced herself with her card:

MISS KNOW IT ALL

Geography   History   Arithmetic
Science   Spelling
Recipes, Riddles, and Weather Reports
Reasonable Rates

Then she had come in and answered questions about everything the Good Day girls could think to ask. She had told them the Pilgrims came to Plymouth in 1620, and the sun was ninety-three million miles from the earth, and how to tell when a pumpkin pie was done. And much more.

For she truly knew everything. Well, perhaps not quite everything, as it turned out. But then one person can't really know *everything*, as Miss Know It All herself admitted.

Now a whole year had gone by, and Miss Know It All was back again.

"Remember me?" Miss Know It All asked brightly, as Miss Plum swung open the door and Miss Lavender appeared breathlessly at her shoulder.

Miss Plum's thin face broke into a smile. Even her gray bun of hair looked happy. "How could we forget *you*," she said.

Miss Lavender peeked around from behind Miss Plum and said, "Hello, Miss Know It All."

"Have you still got your box of candy?" someone asked, a tiny voice from the midst of the crowd of girls.

Everyone grew silent and looked to see who had spoken. And there, close to Miss Know It All, stood Little Ann, the very smallest of all the Good Day girls. Her round, jam-spotted face was turned up to Miss Know It All. "Have you still got it?"

"Have you? Have you?" The other girls remembered Miss Know It All's box of candy just as well as Little Ann did. They watched with joy as Miss Know It All reached into her coat pocket and drew out the box.

"Let's pass this around while we talk," she said, and followed Miss Plum and Miss Lavender down the hall to the parlor.

"Yoo-hoo," said Cook from the kitchen door.

"Miss Know It All came back," Mary called to Cook.

"She can see that for herself." Elsie May poked Mary, but Mary didn't mind.

"Miss Know It All came back, Miss Know It All came back—" It was like a refrain from a poem, a poem Mary herself might write one day soon.

"Yoo-hoo, yourself." Miss Know It All waved cheerily at Cook as she went into the parlor and settled herself in a comfy spot on the sofa. She was pleased to see a small fire burning on the hearth, for the spring air had a chill today. She held her hands toward the fire and rubbed them together contentedly.

The candy box went around from hand to hand as the girls sat down. When there were no more chairs, they sat cross-legged on the floor. The candy box was not very big, but as it passed from girl to girl, it never became empty. And when it had been all around to everyone there was still just as much candy in it as before. It was the kind of candy box every girl wished she had for her very own!

Things were just the same as always. Miss Know It All would answer the questions, and maybe she would play her music box, as she had done before, and show them the picture of her handsome brother, Albert Know It All. And maybe she would pass around the wonderful box of candy once again.

Miss Know It All unbuttoned her coat and settled back against the sofa cushions.

"I'm so glad to be here again," she said, smiling around at all the girls and at Miss Plum and Miss Lavender. "I have a problem and I know you are just the ones to help me. That's why I've come—for your help."

"Why, of course," said Miss Plum, speaking for all. "We'll help you in any way we can."

"I knew you would," said Miss Know It All.

"But how can *we* help *you*?" Miss Lavender asked with surprise. Miss Know It All knew so much more than everybody else, it seemed odd to Miss Lavender that there was any problem Miss Know It All could not handle.

"I'm not sure yet," Miss Know It All replied thoughtfully. "But I just felt I should come to Butterfield Square—that somehow the answer would be here."

2

The Strange Gift

"What is your problem?" Miss Plum asked kindly.

Everyone grew very still, every eye upon Miss Know It All. Even Tatty, licking the last of a smudge of chocolate candy from her fingers, kept her eyes upon Miss Know It All at the same time so she wouldn't miss anything.

Miss Know It All looked around at all

the friendly faces turned her way. It made her feel very, very good.

"Just a few days ago I received an unexpected package in the mail," she began. As she spoke, she opened her big black pocketbook and took out a small white cardboard box. She held it out for everyone to see.

"It was well wrapped up in brown mailing paper," Miss Know It All continued, "and tied with string. And it had a stamp with a picture of the queen of England. My name was very carefully printed on the wrapper. But there was no other name, or any other clue as to who had sent the package."

Miss Know It All paused a moment, looking around at everyone. "But that wasn't the strangest part."

"It wasn't?" Miss Lavender said.

Miss Know It All shook her head. "No, indeed. The strangest part was not knowing what the package was—or, to put it another way, what was inside the package."

She opened the white box and held it so that everyone could see. It was full of small brightly colored objects, smooth and nearly round, like colored stones, or pills, perhaps.

"What are they?" Tatty asked.

"My words exactly," said Miss Know It All. "When I had admired the queen's picture on the stamp, and undid the string and unwrapped the brown paper, I opened this box and said to myself, 'What are they?' But there was no one to answer me. I live alone, you know."

"Doesn't your brother Albert live with you?" Miss Lavender asked.

"Albert travels almost all the time," Miss Know It All explained. She sighed faintly and smiled. "It does make me lonesome sometimes. But he has a wanderlust. Some men do."

Miss Lavender and Miss Plum nodded gravely, and all the little girls looked sad.

"But, of course, I travel a lot myself,"

Miss Know It All went on more brightly. "It's my line of work, to share my knowledge, to get about and answer people's questions. Albert does the same, only he comes home much more rarely than I do. As a matter of fact, speaking of Albert, I hope you won't mind but I've sent a message to him—I think he is traveling in Africa right now—but anyway, I've sent him a message to meet me here. Albert may be able to help us solve this problem."

"All the way from Africa?" Miss Plum asked in amazement. "He would come all the way from Africa?"

"It wouldn't take him a moment," Miss Know It All assured Miss Plum. "Travel is very easy for Albert. He comes and goes like a breath of air—well, you'll see for yourselves when he arrives."

Little Ann had lost track of the conversation. Now she reached out curiously to touch the shiny little things in the white box.

"Are they good to eat?" she asked.

"Land sakes, no!" Miss Know It All quickly drew the box away from Little Ann. "Never eat strange things."

"Remember what happened to Alice," Mary said to Little Ann.

"Alice who?" asked Little Ann.

"Alice in Wonderland," Mary replied wisely.

"Yes, that's right," Miss Plum agreed. "You wouldn't want to shrink down and slide under the door, would you?"

"Or get so big your head came through the roof and all your arms and legs stuck out the doors and windows," said Elsie May.

Everyone grew very solemn and looked again at the box Miss Know It All was holding.

"Well, to get back to my story," Miss Know It All said suddenly, "after I had unwrapped the package and opened the box and said, 'What are they?' there was no one

16

to tell me. I did not know what these things were then, and I thought about it for several days and I still did not know, even though my name is Miss Know It All. One person can't really know *every*thing, as we all learned when I was here before."

"But you know a great many things," Miss Lavender said consolingly. "You mustn't feel badly over one or two things you don't know."

"I suppose you're right," Miss Know It All agreed. She smiled at Miss Lavender. The bright little pebbles, or pills, or candies, or whatever-they-weres, rattled together as she jiggled the box.

Every girl stared at them and wondered if she ate one would she, like Alice, slide under doors or grow big enough to fill up a whole house.

But no one was brave enough to try— even if Miss Plum and Miss Lavender and Miss Know It All would have let them.

And as far as the ladies were concerned, no one was going to eat one of those things just to find out what it was! There would have to be some other way.

3

Mr. Not So Much

Just then there was a loud knocking at the front door. A loud crash at the door would perhaps describe it better, for the door trembled on its hinges and the whole house seemed to shudder.

In the kitchen Cook dropped a pan on her toe because she was so startled. But she knew right away who was knocking. No one else knocked at the door like *that*.

Once a month one of the members of the Board of Directors of The Good Day, a stern, tightfisted man named Mr. Not So Much, came pounding at the door in just this manner. When he was admitted he would stride down the hall to the parlor, little girls scattering left and right along the way if they were unfortunate enough to be in the hallway at the time. Then Mr. Not So Much would remove his hat and gloves and sit in the parlor with Miss Lavender and Miss Plum and go over the monthly bills and say:

"Not so much for groceries.

"Not so much for shoes.

"Not so much for this and not so much for that—"

He could not seem to teach Miss Plum and Miss Lavender that they must not spend money.

"I'd like to see him keep twenty-eight girls in clean dresses and warm coats without spending any money," Miss Plum would

20

say to Miss Lavender when Mr. Not So Much had gone.

"So would I," Miss Lavender would agree. She always agreed with Miss Plum.

Mr. Not So Much was as glad as Miss Plum and Miss Lavender when the monthly visit was over. He looked forward to it as little as they did, and this spring afternoon was no exception. He stood at the door, already frowning terribly over the occasion, a thin man with a thin face and a pocket watch hung at the end of a long gold chain. Mr. Not So Much consulted his watch frequently during his talks with Miss Plum and Miss Lavender. Time was another thing he did not like to spend too much of, and he would glare at the face of his watch from time to time as if to stop the hands from turning around to count off the minutes and hours.

He lifted his hand to knock again and almost hit Cook, who had come running from the kitchen to open the door.

In the parlor, where the first knocking had been plainly heard, one of the girls said, "Maybe that's Albert."

But Miss Know It All shook her head. "Albert doesn't knock on doors," she said.

Before there was time to explain further, Mr. Not So Much appeared in the parlor doorway, his lips pressed tight together with disapproval on seeing so many people occupying the room where he had thought to see only Miss Plum and Miss Lavender.

"Come in, Mr. Not So Much." Miss Plum rose from her chair and began to shoo little girls out of the room ... Tatty and Kate and red-haired Mary ... Elsie May with her turned-up nose ... Little Ann with jam *and* chocolate candy on her face ... and all the rest. They went reluctantly, looking back over their shoulders to wave to Miss Know It All.

When the last girl had left, Miss Plum said to Mr. Not So Much, "You remember

Miss Know It All, who visited us last spring."

Mr. Not So Much looked down at Miss Know It All without enthusiasm. Another mouth to feed! he was thinking. How long would *she* stay.

"How do you do, Madam," he said stiffly, giving no sign whether or not he recalled her from last spring. Surely, he was hoping, she would not turn up every year.

Miss Know It All set the white cardboard box on the table by the sofa, and held out her hand.

Mr. Not So Much took it grimly and gave it a shake. Then he stood with some impatience, hands clasped behind his back, chin sunk upon his chest.

"Mr. Not So Much has come to see about the monthly expenses," Miss Lavender whispered to Miss Know It All.

"Of course," Miss Know It All said graciously. "You must get on with your business at once. I think I'll go out to the kitchen and chat with Cook for a while." She rose from the sofa, leaving a soft depression where she had been sitting.

"If you wouldn't mind," Miss Plum said gratefully.

"No, I don't mind at all." Miss Know It All took up her pocketbook. "So nice to meet you again, Mr. Not So Much."

"Ummmm," Mr. Not So Much mumbled. The mention of Cook and the kitchen always sent him into a state of despair. For in the kitchen Cook put raisins in the muffins and frosting on the cake and jam on the crackers—and all sorts of unnecessary *expensive* things! Cook and her kitchen were, in fact, some of Mr. Not So Much's biggest problems. He felt that he was getting a headache now that Miss Know It All had reminded him about Cook and the kitchen.

When Miss Know It All went out, Mr. Not So Much followed Miss Plum gloomily

to her desk in one corner of the room. He saw that a fire was burning behind the grate. A fire in springtime! His headache grew worse. Money to burn, that's what Miss Plum and Miss Lavender thought they had.

Miss Lavender, who did not have much to do with the bills, tried to make herself very small and unseen in another part of the room. She got out her sewing basket and picked out the oldest, most worn little dress that had to be mended and began to work on that, so Mr. Not So Much could see how hard they always tried to save money.

In the kitchen Cook was preparing a tea tray. She had not expected Mr. Not So Much and she had already put some lovely straw-berry tarts on it. Now she removed the tarts and put a few thin, dry crackers on the tray.

When Miss Know It All saw this, she said she would have her tea in the kitchen with the strawberry tarts.

Cook put on her most serious and humble face, and carried the tray into the parlor.

But by that time, Mr. Not So Much was too upset about the monthly expenses to notice what was on the tray.

"Ladies, ladies, when will you learn—" he was saying, flourishing in his hand the bill from the hardware store for six pairs of roller skates.

"What is springtime without roller skates?" Miss Lavender protested timidly.

"And *this*." Mr. Not So Much held up another bill—a bill for twenty-eight pairs of new shoes. *Twenty-eight pairs*. Mr. Not So Much could hardly believe his eyes. "More shoes? We just bought shoes last year."

"But girls outgrow their shoes," Miss Plum said.

"And they were wearing through at the soles," Miss Lavender said.

Mr. Not So Much stared at the ladies. "Outgrown? Wearing out already?" It seemed he could never win. Twenty-eight

27

girls went through an amazing amount of shoes and coats and mittens and dresses. Weakly, Mr. Not So Much took up another bill.

Cook set down the tea tray and said, "Tea is served."

"How nice—" Miss Plum started to say, but Mr. Not So Much had seized another bill and held it close to his bony face to study it. He could really hardly believe this bill. It was for twelve pairs of dancing slippers—*dancing slippers!* It might as well have been for twelve tickets to the moon.

In desperation Mr. Not So Much glanced down and saw on the table beside the tea tray a box of bright-colored little pills. They looked so much like the pills he took when business pressures distressed him that without thinking he reached down and took one from the box and popped it into his mouth.

4

"More Laughter, More Singing"

Miss Plum and Miss Lavender both opened their mouths at once to cry out—"Wait! Stop!" But they were too late. Into Mr. Not So Much's mouth went one of the strange things from Miss Know It All's white cardboard box. And the ladies sat aghast.

But not for long.

Almost at once Mr. Not So Much realized his mistake, for this did not taste like his usual pills. He spit it out into the palm of his hand and tossed it into the fire.

The flames flared upward for a moment, and a great black cloud of smoke billowed out into the parlor—and then the fire was gone. Not even a glowing ember remained.

Miss Plum and Miss Lavender and Cook stared in speechless amazement at the fireplace. But before they could wonder too long about what had happened to their lovely fire, other events took place that were cause for even more amazement.

Mr. Not So Much said, "Ladies, shall we have our tea?" His voice was soothing and gentle; his face wore a magnificent smile from cheek to cheek. His dark eyes glowed with kindness.

He had seated himself on the sofa and was looking at the tea tray and the plate of dry crackers.

"Now, now, now," he said, rubbing his

hands together pleasantly, "let's have something more appetizing than this, Cook." He
smiled up at her fondly. "Haven't you got
some of those delicious cakes you make,
with frosting and nuts? Or some raisin muffins, perhaps?"

"I—I have some strawberry tarts," Cook
managed to stammer. She picked up the
plate of crackers and backed out into the hall.
Even then she did not go straight away to the
kitchen, but remained peeking into the parlor from the side of the doorway to see what
would happen next.

What happened next was that Mr. Not
So Much noticed the fire was no longer burning.

"Why, I see the fire has gone out,
ladies," he declared, and stood up at once
and added another log. He struck a match
and he soon had a full roaring fire again, indeed so bright and hot that Miss Lavender
and Miss Plum began to feel warm. But Mr.

31

Not So Much did not stop there. He noticed some little girls going by in the hall, and he called to them, "Come in, girls, come in and sing me a song. That's what we want, isn't it, ladies?" He smiled at the stunned Miss Plum and Miss Lavender. "That's what we want, ladies—more laughter, more singing."

Cook fled to the kitchen, the plate of crackers shaking in her hand.

"Why, whatever is the matter?" Miss Know It All asked, her mouth full of strawberry tart.

"Oh—it's him, it's him—" Cook could hardly get her wits together to make a complete sentence.

Miss Know It All swallowed down her strawberry tart with a sip of tea, and stepped briskly out into the hall to see what she could see. There was nothing to see in the hall, which was deserted now, as the girls had been coaxed into the parlor and were being led by Mr. Not So Much in a medley of songs:

"Oh, Susanna! Oh, don't you cry for me—" Mr. Not So Much's voice rose the loudest and strongest of them all.

When he got the girls singing along well, Mr. Not So Much flitted on to other things. "More lamps lit," he suggested, going from lamp to lamp about the parlor until the room was ablaze with light. "More wood on the fire—more sugar for the tea . . . speaking of tea, where is Cook? We want some tarts now that the girls are here. Yes, indeed, some tarts and cakes and candies." And he started out of the parlor, still beating time for the singers, who were now on the last chorus and had begun to screech rather loudly:

"For I've come from A-la-bam-a, with my ban-jo on my knee!"

Miss Lavender covered her ears and moved farther away from the heat of the raging fire.

Miss Plum stood blinking like an owl in the flood of electric lights.

"Pardon me, my dear!" Mr. Not So

33

Much, on his way to find Cook, nearly ran into Miss Know It All, who stood by the parlor doorway gazing upon this strange scene. He patted her arm gently and said, "Come in and have tea with us. I'm just on my way to the kitchen to tell Cook how many we have here. Lots of tarts will be needed."

"Yes, I can see that," Miss Know It All answered faintly. Eight little girls stood by the sofa, singing and perspiring in the heat from the fire.

Before she could say more, Mr. Not So Much—who ordinarily disapproved of everything from electric light bills to children who made noise—had disappeared through the kitchen door in search of tarts and cakes with frosting and muffins with raisins.

Miss Know It All closed her eyes and sighed a deep, deep sigh—partly to recover from the rather breathtaking events, partly in relief. Now she knew what was in the package she had received in the mail.

36

The small brightly colored objects were indeed pills—to be taken and eaten up. They were "Other-Way-Around" pills, and she wondered with a sudden sense of panic how many Mr. Not So Much had eaten!

5

Albert Arrives

At the same moment that Miss Know It All realized what had happened and what the pills were, she also realized who had sent them to her. All her mysteries were solved at once.

She stepped into the parlor, where Miss Plum and Miss Lavender and the eight girls—who had finally stopped singing—were faced with the unexpected arrival of Albert Know It All. He suddenly appeared in a chair beside the roaring fireplace.

He had come straight from Africa and did not mind the heat.

The girls drew together in a mingled state of surprise and fright to see someone appear without warning in a chair that had been empty the moment before.

Miss Plum and Miss Lavender, hardly less taken aback, peered at this newcomer.

"Who are you?" Miss Plum managed to ask. Her voice did not sound quite right, and she cleared her throat and coughed.

"Why—aren't you Miss Know It All's brother?" Miss Lavender murmured. She thought she recognized Albert from the picture Miss Know It All carried.

"At your service." Albert Know It All rose courteously from the chair and made a bow from the waist in the direction of Miss Plum and Miss Lavender and the eight little girls.

He was every bit as handsome as his photograph—they could see that at once. His hair was very dark and curly, and he had a mustache and bright twinkling eyes. He wore an African safari suit, pith helmet, boots and all. In his belt he carried a knife for hacking through the jungles, and his arms were burned by the African sun.

"Albert!" Miss Know It All called, coming across the parlor and into his arms. "How happy I am to see you."

Albert hugged Miss Know It All and kissed her on the cheek. Miss Lavender thought it was very sweet.

"I'm so glad you could come, Albert," Miss Know It All said. "These are my friends, Miss Lavender and Miss Plum—and you must meet the girls, too. Come here, girls—" And one by one, she introduced Elsie May, with long yellow braids and blue hairbows; Tatty, with her stockings down again and a shoe unbuckled; Mary, with a

notebook in her pocket to write poems; Elizabeth, who was very, very pretty; Nonnie, who was plump and wise; Kate, who wished she were a boy; Phoebe, who could blow the biggest bubbles with her gum; and Little Ann, who was only six and a half years old.

"Well, well, well," Albert said. "Such lovely girls, such lovely girls."

"Now, Albert—about why you've come—" Miss Know It All had taken up the white cardboard box and held it toward Albert. She was about to tell him what had occurred, but he spoke before she could continue.

"Why, those are 'Other-Way-Around' pills." One glance had been enough for Albert to tell. "I hope nobody's been fooling with them," he added soberly.

He looked around at the girls with a worried expression. "'Other-Way-Around' pills are nothing to fool with."

The girls all began to shake their heads.

"I know *now* what they are," Miss Know It All said to Albert, "but I just found out a moment ago. Mr. Not So Much ate one, and he's—well—" Her voice drifted off.

Albert looked very interested. "He's gone the other-way-around?"

"I'm afraid so," Miss Know It All answered.

"Oh, my, my, my." Miss Lavender felt faint. She sat down in a heap on the sofa.

Miss Plum quieted the little girls, who were beginning to whisper among themselves. "Let me understand this," she said. "Mr. Not So Much has eaten one of these pills and—"

"Only part of one," Miss Lavender murmured faintly from the sofa.

"Yes, that's right, only part of one," Miss Plum agreed. "He threw what was left of the pill into the fire, and the fire went out."

"Naturally," said Albert with an elegant

and handsome shrug. "Even fires can go the other-way-around."

"Will Mr. Not So Much always be like this from now on?" Miss Plum asked. She was not sure whether she could bear all the goodwill, the fires, lights, festivity, and noise any easier than she had borne the director's penny-pinching sermons and angry words.

"It depends on how many he has eaten," Albert said matter-of-factly. "If, as you say, he only took one and didn't even eat all of that, why, the effects will probably be very short-lasting—"

He was interrupted by the arrival of Mr. Not So Much himself, who advanced into the parlor slowly, shaking his head as though he had just wakened from sleep.

"Why—what's this, ladies? Lamps on in the middle of the day? It's still broad daylight outside. How can you be so extravagant?"

He went from lamp to lamp turning them off. When Little Ann started to whisper something to Tatty, Mr. Not So Much swung about sharply and cried, "Not so much noise there!"

And at the sound of this old familiar voice, Cook, coming along the hall from the kitchen with a tray ladened with strawberry tarts and chocolate cookies, did a complete about-face and went back into the kitchen for her plate of thin, dry crackers.

It seemed that their question was plainly answered. Mr. Not So Much had not had a very big dose of other-way-aroundness. He was already over it, in fact, and quite his usual self again—which was rather a pity, of course. But at least now everybody knew what to expect from him.

6

Miss Know It All
Writes a Letter

Mr. Not So Much did not stay any longer. He did not even stay to have a cup of tea and a thin cracker. He had had all he could stand for one day of Miss Plum's monthly bills, fires burning away merrily (money going up in smoke to his way of thinking), and children standing around outgrowing their shoes moment by moment.

He put on his hat, bade everyone good-bye, and left. He strode off into the afternoon. Above his head a clap of thunder sounded and a rising wind tugged at his coat and forced him to hold onto his hat or lose it. Soon he was out of sight, as the first drops of the sudden spring storm spattered the ground.

In the parlor Miss Know It All drew up a chair next to Albert's and the two put their heads together.

"It could only be that wicked William Wise who sent them to me, don't you agree, Albert?" Miss Know It All said.

"Yes," Albert admitted. He twirled his handsome mustache. "I think we must say it was William. Dear William hasn't given up yet."

Albert tweaked Miss Know It All's cheek, and she blushed and said, "Now be serious, Albert. *Dear* William, my foot!"

"Who is William?" Tatty asked. She tugged at Miss Know It All's skirt to get her attention.

Miss Plum thought perhaps she ought

47

to remind Tatty that it was not polite to ask questions that did not concern her. But Miss Plum herself was curious to know who William Wise was and why he had sent such a strange gift to Miss Know It All.

Miss Know It All put her arm around Tatty and drew her close to the chair. The other girls edged closer, too, and Little Ann came up the closest of all and sat down on the floor by Miss Know It All's shoes.

"William Wise is a very smart man," Miss Know It All explained first. "If you think Albert and I know a lot of things, you should meet William Wise! He is a walking encyclopedia all by himself."

The girls listened eagerly. Miss Plum sat down beside Miss Lavender on the sofa and they listened, too.

"Albert and I have known William since we were all children together," Miss Know It All continued, "and he is the wisest of the three of us."

"And he has always been very fond of my sister," Albert took up the story. "Always wanted her to settle down and marry him, and stop going around the world answering questions for people. He has often said to me, 'Albert, it would be so nice if your sister was just an ordinary woman instead of a Know It All.'"

"And that's why he sent me these pills," Miss Know It All said. "It is so plain now— oh, but such a wicked, wicked thing to do.

"You see," she explained to Tatty and the other girls, "if I had eaten the pills I would have gone the other-way-around, like Mr. Not So Much did. I would have become very dumb. I wouldn't know anything at all. Then, William probably thought, I would be happy to settle down and be Mrs. William Wise."

"Dumb Mrs. William Wise," Albert corrected her.

"Yes," Miss Know It All repeated, "dumb Mrs. William Wise."

"Dumb Mrs. William Wise," Miss Plum could not help echoing. It certainly had an extraordinary sound.

"He would probably have put an "Other-Way-Around" pill in my tea every morning," Miss Know It All concluded. "What a wicked scheme."

She brooded about this a bit. "I think I will just write to him," she decided abruptly. "I'll write to him and demand an apology for this shabby trick, this wicked gift."

"A good idea," Albert said. And with a twirl of his mustache he disappeared from the chair.

"He's *gone!*" all the girls cried out at once.

"Pay no attention to him," Miss Know It All said with a wave of her hand. "He's inclined to be a bit of a show-off with his comings and goings. I suppose he's back in Africa by now, studying birdcalls and plant life."

"Oh, dear," said Miss Lavender a little

wistfully, "I was hoping he would stay for supper and tell us some of his adventures."

But Miss Know It All did not seem to hear. She got up from her chair and seemed to be composing the letter to William Wise in her head. After a moment she said, "May I have a pen and paper, please?"

Miss Plum got these at once from her desk.

Miss Know It All wrote a letter to William Wise asking him to come to her without delay, and in person, to apologize for his actions.

"May I ask him to come here?" Miss Know It All asked.

"Yes, please do," said Miss Plum. Who would pass up the chance to meet Wicked William Wise?

Miss Know It All finished the letter promptly. She stuck on a stamp with a sharp rap of her clenched fist—as though she were smacking William Wise's head. Then she ad-

dressed the envelope to "Wicked William Wise." She underlined the word "wicked" so that he would quickly see the state of her mind and understand that she did not want any excuses.

"Now," said Miss Know It All, "when the rain stops we'll get this letter out to the nearest mailbox."

And then she laughed and stood up. "On second thought, we will not have to wait for the rain to stop."

She took the white cardboard box, marched down the hall, flung open the front door, and tossed an "Other-Way-Around" pill into the air—and then another, and another. When three or four had flown off across the yard, the rain stopped and the sun came out—and Elsie May (the oldest Good Day girl) was sent off to mail the letter to "*Wicked* William Wise."

7

Miss Know It All's Hiccup Cures

It would be several days before William Wise could be expected, for he did not have Albert's speedy way of traveling. So Miss Know It All settled down for a nice visit with all her friends in Butterfield Square.

She shared with Cook many new recipes she had acquired on her worldwide trips, and she answered all the questions the Good Day girls asked her.

"Who invented gum?" Phoebe wanted to know. To her it was a staple of life.

"William Semple of Mount Vernon, Ohio, was granted the first patent for chewing gum in the nineteenth century," Miss Know It All replied without hesitation. "I think that would qualify him to be considered its inventor."

Miss Plum sighed deeply. Sometimes— seeing one Good Day girl or another lost from sight behind a pink bubble of gum— Miss Plum was not sure that William Semple of Mount Vernon, Ohio, had done anybody any favor.

"How hot is the sun?" asked a girl named Agnes, who was very studious.

"Sixteen million degrees centigrade at its center," Miss Know It All answered cheerfully.

"How old is the moon?"

"It is said to be four and a half billion years old."

Agnes could go on and on forever with scientific questions, but Little Ann was waving her hand for attention. Miss Know It All thought it should be her turn now.

"What is it, Little Ann?" Miss Know It All said.

"When will a white dog come into your house?" Little Ann asked. Everybody laughed and pretended to be dismayed, for they all remembered another time when someone has asked Miss Know It All a riddle.

"A white dog will come into your house when the door is open," Miss Know It All said, giving Little Ann a pat on her head.

When Miss Know It All was not giving Cook recipes or answering questions for the girls, she occupied her time with a book she was writing. It was to be called, "Miss Know It All's Almanac of Assorted Facts, Recipes, Cures, and Remedies."

It included eighty-seven cures for hiccups, recipes for invisible ink and watermelon pie, remedies for gloomy days and fingernail-biting, and many other things of great interest.

One day Kate had hiccups, and Miss Know It All ran down her list of cures one by one:

Kate stuck her head in a paper bag. The hiccups did not stop.

"I can hear her hiccuping in there," Elsie May announced with authority.

They pulled Kate's head out of the paper bag, and gave her a spoonful of sugar to hold on her tongue.

Kate swallowed the sugar quickly and asked for more. "That was very good," said Kate between hiccups.

She tried to drink water while holding her fingers in her ears—and the front of her dress got all spattered—but the hiccups were not disturbed a bit.

She tried counting to one hundred while she held her breath, but she kept hiccuping and then she would have to start over. Finally she gave that up.

She tried to touch her nose with her tongue. She made a dreadful face doing this, and she never did reach her nose. And the hiccups did not stop.

She turned around in a circle ten times. And got very dizzy.

She tried to say "Jack Sprat Could Eat No Fat" backward, and got all mixed up before she said the first line.

But when she reached number eight on Miss Know It All's list, she was cured. She tried to hold her nose with one hand and her tongue with the other and sing "The Star Spangled Banner"—and she was cured.

Everyone agreed that Miss Know It All's hiccup cures alone were enough to make her book a big success.

So one by one the days passed by. Everyone waited eagerly and curiously—and a little bit fearfully—to see what Wicked William Wise would be like.

"I bet he'll have horns growing right out of his head, like this." Phoebe demonstrated by holding her fingers up above her head like two stiff horns.

"He'll be very mean and sinister looking," Elsie May said—"with a sly smile and long fingernails."

Little Ann drew closer to Tatty when she heard this.

"When he opens his mouth, out will come fire—like a dragon," Phoebe went on, prancing around wiggling her horns.

"And he'll come in and leer around at everyone, and then reach out and scratch someone with his long fingernails. That's how he keeps them sharp," Elsie May continued.

"He'll have all kinds of wicked, horrible pills in his pockets," Mary said. "And he'll go up and down the street pretending to be kind and offering everybody his pills."

"And he probably has a tail, like a dragon," Phoebe said.

"And he has a whip to beat the children," said Elsie May.

Mary wrote a poem called "Wicked William Wise."

> Wicked William Wise
> Has six yellow eyes
> And a brain full of pies
> That he cannot disguise.

"That makes about as much sense as—as—" Elsie May fumbled for words and finished triumphantly "—as if a two-year-old had written it!"

"Thank you," said Mary, unruffled. "You are very sweet."

They thought the days would never pass until Wicked William Wise would come.

8

Wicked William Wise

Toward the end of the week, on Thursday afternoon to be exact, the Good Day girls were returning from school. They were strung out along the sidewalk in twos and threes, hair flying, coats unbuttoned—despite all of Miss Lavender's reminders to button up—and they passed a roly-poly gentleman strolling along toward Butterfield Square, his nose in a book. He hardly no-

ticed the girls race by him, although twenty-
eight girls make a considerable amount of
commotion when they are set free of school
and are on their way to a good snack in
Cook's kitchen.

And they in turn hardly noticed the
roly-poly little man—except for perhaps
Agnes. She noticed him because she did not
often see people walking along the street
reading a book, and she thought that it
looked like something she might try herself
one day.

All the girls ran past and way ahead of
the gentleman book-reader. Indeed, they
were soon out of sight altogether as they disappeared up the walk and into the door of
Number 18.

Unhurried, the gentleman finished the
page he was on, closed his book, and put a
monocle to his eye. He was looking for a cer-
tain house number. When he reached the
gate at Number 18 he put the monocle into

his pocket. Then, still carefully holding the rather large book under one arm, he took off his hat and ran his sleeve around the brim to dust it off, although it was as clean and bright as everything else he wore.

He replaced the hat upon his head and proceeded up the walk so recently pounded over by twenty-eight hungry girls.

In the parlor the clock was striking the quarter hour, and Miss Plum was seating herself at the piano. It was Nonnie's piano lesson time. Almost at once Nonnie appeared, a smear of pink frosting on one corner of her mouth—though not for long, as she put out her tongue and licked it away. Then she sat down on the piano stool and looked sweetly at the music before her. She had not practiced much this week, but she was hoping to do her best.

Miss Lavender was busy with the mending, a never-ending job with twenty-eight little girls. Miss Know It All was at work on her book, composing a section on decorating paper plates in the "Remedies for Rainy Days" chapter.

Miss Lavender was the first to hear the very, very soft rap at the front door.

She lifted her head from her sewing, but Nonnie was in the middle of a scale and Miss Lavender could not be sure she had really heard a rap.

But, yes. Just as Nonnie finished the scale and paused, the rap came again, more distinctly now. Even Miss Know It All heard it, and looked up from her writing.

"Is that someone at the door?" she asked Miss Lavender.

"Yes," said Miss Lavender, "I believe it is."

Miss Lavender got up and went out of the parlor quietly so as not to disturb the music lesson. Tick-tick-tick went the metronome. Tap-tap-tap went Miss Plum's fingers on the side of the piano, keeping time.

Miss Know It All put down her pen and turned toward the parlor door as Miss Lavender returned. Forgetting the piano lesson now, Miss Lavender announced with some excitement, "Mr. William Wise has arrived!"

There he stood, plump and pink-cheeked, hat in hand, very neat with polished shoes and a sparkling tiepin, and a handkerchief folded in his breast pocket. Under his arm was the book: *Centurion Encyclopedia, Vol. 9.*

Miss Plum and Nonnie turned from the piano at the sound of his name.

Every eye in the room was now upon him, but Wicked William Wise looked only at Miss Know It All. He hung back shyly in the doorway, and Miss Lavender had to coax him to come farther into the parlor.

Tatty and Mary were going by in the hall. When they heard Miss Lavender say that William Wise had arrived, they ran off at once to get all the other girls to come and see!

"William, I would like you to meet my friends, Miss Lavender and Miss Plum and Nonnie."

Miss Plum rose from her chair by the piano, and Nonnie never did have her lesson *that* day. She hovered half out of sight behind the piano, staring at Wicked William Wise, and by and by, as Tatty and Mary spread the word, heads began to appear at the parlor doorway—heads with wide little-girl eyes and little-girl mouths making *Oh*'s of surprise.

"Well, William, how do you explain this miserable trick?" Miss Know It All's voice grew considerably more brusque when she had completed the introductions and William Wise had been lured into the parlor.

"What trick, my dear? Me? A trick?" He fumbled for words. He was obviously very

much upset to think that Miss Know It All was angry with him.

"*This* trick," Miss Know It All reminded him, shoving the box of "Other-Way-Around" pills under his nose.

He drew back quietly, flushing with embarrassment.

"Oh, that," he echoed lamely.

"Yes," Miss Know It All repeated emphatically, "*that!*"

"*But, my dear—*" He twisted his hat and looked more wretched than ever. The little girls began to feel pangs of sympathy for him. He did not look wicked at all now that he was here, although Phoebe was disappointed that he didn't have at least some tiny horns.

"Don't 'my dear' me," Miss Know It All reprimanded him. "You're too old for such foolishness, William. And you should know better. If you know anything, you should know better."

72

"You are quite right," William Wise's voice faded away. Everyone waited, but he did not say anything more. It seemed, in fact, that he was reading the label on a box of paper clips which was on the table where Miss Know It All had been writing. Then he began to read the loose pages of her book, which she suddenly snatched from the table and held behind her back out of sight.

"I'd forgotten"—she explained to Miss Plum and Miss Lavender—"William can't help reading everything he sees. Labels, small print nobody else bothers with, street signs, want ads, everything—oh, there he goes again."

William Wise was reading a shopping list that Miss Plum had made out for Cook.

"William! Pay attention to me now." Miss Know It All took away the shopping list.

"I'm sorry." The roly-poly man shifted

his encyclopedia apologetically. "And I truly am sorry you didn't like my gift."

"To say the least," Miss Know It All retorted.

William Wise had nothing to say in his defense.

"I thought it was only right that you come and make amends to me," Miss Know It All continued. "You wanted me to take those pills and forget everything I knew. You wanted me to be a—a Miss Know Nothing."

William Wise nodded unhappily. He did seem extremely sorry for what he had done, because it had upset Miss Know It All.

He cast an embarrassed glance about the room, and finally, despite the disadvantage of such a large audience, he blurted out at last—"I was driven to it."

"Humph!" Miss Know It All muttered to herself. "Such shenanigans."

(Little Ann looked around hopefully, but she did not see any "shenanigans" in the parlor. She thought they were probably elves or fairies.)

William Wise hung his head sadly.

"Well," said Miss Plum, rising and smoothing her skirt, "it must be close to suppertime. Will you have supper with us. Mr. Wise?"

"Why, yes, I will," he answered gratefully. At least there was *someone* who was not mad at him.

He spent the time until supper was served reading his encyclopedia in a corner of the parlor.

9

The Last Evening

Supper that night was a very strange affair, for Cook had outdone herself on recipes that Miss Know It All had provided.

Miss Plum and Miss Lavender approached each new dish with caution. In fact, Miss Lavender was not at all sure most of the time what it was she was eating. But Miss Know It All relished everything, and complimented Cook by telling her that she had prepared every recipe to perfection.

Cook's face was wreathed in smiles, and she bustled about as perky as a girl.

The twenty-eight children loved everything that was served—except for one or two girls who had been at the cookie jar before supper and were too full to eat anything more.

When the dessert had been served, William Wise consented to tell the Butterfield Square girls about his own boyhood, and what it had been like growing up so wise.

"I knew when storms were coming," William Wise told the little girls, "and that is very handy. I knew what days to wear my overshoes, and what day in spring to leave off my long winter underwear."

"You knew everything in every book in the town library, didn't you, William?" Miss Know It All said. A note of pride could be heard in her voice. When she was not exasperated with William Wise for wanting her to be dumb, she was rather pleased that he was so wise.

"I knew why the crickets chirped," said William Wise.

"And why flies buzzed. And why moss was green.

"If I read something once, I never forgot it.

"I won all the spelling bees. There was not a word I could not spell."

"Think of *that*, Tatty." Miss Plum could not help smiling gently. Tatty had a lot of trouble with spelling. When she was not sure about a word she always put in a lot of letters, hoping to hit on the right ones.

"Once I won an ivory letter opener in a spelling contest," Mr. Wise said with modest satisfaction.

"Real ivory?" Miss Lavender asked.

"Yes, indeed," said William Wise. "It was from the tusk of an elephant, you know."

"My, my." Miss Lavender thought that sounded very exciting. Imagine opening the morning mail with a letter opener carved from the tusk of an elephant from far-off Africa or India!

As there were no accommodations for Mr. Wise to spend the night at The Good Day, and he had a train ticket back to his own home, he departed again when supper was over.

Miss Plum and Miss Lavender, Miss Know It All, and all the Good Day girls walked with Mr. Wise to the front gate to say good-bye.

"Good-bye, William," Miss Know It All said. Her expression softened, and she added, "I have no hard feelings."

"I'm so glad, my dear." Mr. Wise shifted his encyclopedia. The little girls pressed closer around to get a good last look at him.

"Good-bye," whispered Little Ann, looking up into his roly-poly pink face.

"Good-bye," said Tatty.

"Good-bye," said Phoebe.

"Good-bye," said Agnes, the studious girl. She gazed with admiration at the man who knew everything.

"Good-bye, Mr. Wise," said Miss Plum.

"Good-bye," said Miss Lavender, her white curls bouncing as she nodded her head. Behind her gold-rimmed spectacles her eyes were brightly fixed upon Mr. William Wise.

"Good-bye," said all the Good Day girls.

"Good-bye," he answered gravely. But he seemed unable to actually go.

"You'll miss your train if you don't get started," Miss Know It All reminded Mr. Wise. He seemed on the point of lingering at the gate for the rest of the evening.

"Yes—yes, you're absolutely right, my dear." He came to his senses, took a firmer grip on his encyclopedia, and lifted his hat in farewell.

Miss Lavender waved her handkerchief,

and the girls hung on the gate and the rails of the black iron fence. Their last sight of him was as he went off down the street, reading his encyclopedia in the gathering twilight.

They saw him pause at the corner to read the lettering on a bakery truck parked at the curb.

MOTHER JONES
Pies and Cakes
Six Kinds of Bread—Baked Fresh Daily
Speedy Delivery
Low Prices—Good Food

What! No buns? William Wise thought to himself, and went on his way reading his encyclopedia.

When the girls had gone to bed, Miss Know It All sat for one last evening with Miss Lavender and Miss Plum in the parlor.

"Tomorrow I must be on my way," she announced.

Miss Plum and Miss Lavender were silent. They knew that Miss Know It All must go, but they wished she could stay.

"Mr. Wise seems like a very nice man," Miss Lavender said at last.

"Yes, he does," Miss Plum agreed. She was sitting in a rocking chair and she pushed against the carpet with her toe and rocked back and forth slowly.

It had grown dark at the windows, and the stars had come out. Upstairs the twenty-eight girls were snug in their beds, asleep. Tomorrow Miss Know It All would pack her pocketbook and go. Maybe she would return again some spring day in the years ahead.

"Yes, William is a nice man in many ways—when he isn't playing his naughty tricks," Miss Know It All admitted. "I wouldn't be surprised if—when the time comes for me to settle down and stop my travels—if I do marry him after all."

Miss Lavender sighed with content-ment. She liked romantic endings.

Miss Plum's thinner, more grave-looking face expressed approval at Miss Know It All's confession.

"He wouldn't be much trouble as a hus-band, I suppose," Miss Plum said. "He'd be reading all the time, I expect."

"I expect," Miss Know It All nodded. "He's been like that ever since he was a boy. Albert often remarked on it."

They were all silent awhile, thinking about Albert in far-off Africa.

Then Miss Know It All picked up the white cardboard box, which had come in the mail, wrapped in brown paper, tied with a string, stamped with a picture of the queen of England, addressed to Miss Know It All— and the cause of her return to Butterfield Square.

"I think I'd like to leave these with you," she said to Miss Plum and Miss Lavender. "I

know you will use them wisely. When you need to go out on a rainy day, or to clear your walk of snow. When your flower vases are empty—"

She dropped a blue pill into an empty vase on the table as she spoke, and the vase was immediately full of beautiful lilacs, purple and white, heavy with sweet perfume.

"Or when your candy dishes are empty—"

She dropped a yellow pill into a bowl on the table, and the bowl was at once the "other-way-around," brimming to the top with gumdrops.

Miss Know It All took up the bowl and passed it around solemnly. Miss Plum and Miss Lavender each took a handful of gumdrops. "Other-Way-Around" pills had some very practical uses.

"I know you will use the pills with discretion," Miss Know It All said, "and not give them to people to eat."

"Now, we wouldn't do that," Miss Lavender said quickly, with a horrified tone of voice.

"No, indeed," said Miss Plum—thinking of Mr. Not So Much running around to find cakes with frosting. That had been a rather interesting experience, she thought; perhaps, after all, easier than struggling with him over the monthly bills. But, no—she resisted the temptation to even think about feeding "Other-Way-Around" pills to Mr. Not So Much.

"We will not give them to people to eat," she assured Miss Know It All.

And so Miss Know It All handed over the white cardboard box to the care and keeping of the ladies of Butterfield Square.

ABOUT THE AUTHOR

CAROL BEACH YORK is a writer with over forty outstanding juvenile and young adult books to her credit, including the popular Bantam titles *Remember Me When I Am Dead, I Will Make You Disappear, Miss Know It All,* and *On That Dark Night.*

Born and raised in Chicago, she began her career writing short stories and sold her first one to *Seventeen* magazine. Her first teen novel, a romance, *Sparrow Lake,* was published in 1962. Since then she has contributed many stories and articles to magazines in both the juvenile and adult markets, in addition to her activity as a novelist. She especially enjoys writing suspense stories.

Ms. York lives in Chicago with her daughter, Diana.

FROM THE SPOOKY, EERIE PEN OF JOHN BELLAIRS . . .

☐ **THE CURSE OF THE**   **15429/$2.75**
BLUE FIGURINE

Johnny Dixon knows a lot about ancient Egypt and curses and evil spirits—but when he finds the blue figurine, he actually "sees" a frightening, super-natural world. Even his friend Professor Childermass can't help him!

☐ **THE MUMMY, THE WILL**   **15323/$2.50**
AND THE CRYPT

For months Johnny has been working on a riddle that would lead to a $10,000 reward. Feeling certain that the money is hidden somewhere in the house of a dead man, Johnny goes into his house where a bolt of lightening reveals to him that the house is not quite deserted . . .

☐ **THE SPELL OF THE**   **15357/$2.50**
SORCERER'S SKULL

Johnny Dixon is back, but this time he's not teamed up with Dr. Childermass. That's because his friend, the Professor, has disappeared!

Shop at home
for quality childrens books
and save money, too.

Now you can order books for the whole family from Bantam's latest listing of hundreds of titles including many fine children's books. *And* this special offer gives you an opportunity to purchase a Bantam book for only 50¢. Here's how:

By ordering any five books at the regular price per order, you can also choose any other single book listed (up to $4.95 value) for just 50¢. Some restrictions do apply, so for further details send for Bantam's listing of titles today.

BANTAM BOOKS, INC.
P.O. Box 1006, South Holland, ILL. 60473

Mr./Mrs./Miss/Ms. _____
                 (please print)

Address _____

City_____ State _____ Zip _____
                                         FC(C)—11/85

Printed in the U.S.A.